Bluebell

The Great Honeypot Robbery

Coming Soon – Bluebell and the Missing Mermaid

Dedicated to Sapphire.
These are the further adventures of Bluebell,
her beloved tooth fairy.

Bluebell

The Great Honeypot Robbery

Published in 2021

by Lost Tower Publications.

Lost Tower Publications

Bluebell

The Great Honeypot Robbery

by P.J. Reed

illustrated by Emma Gribble

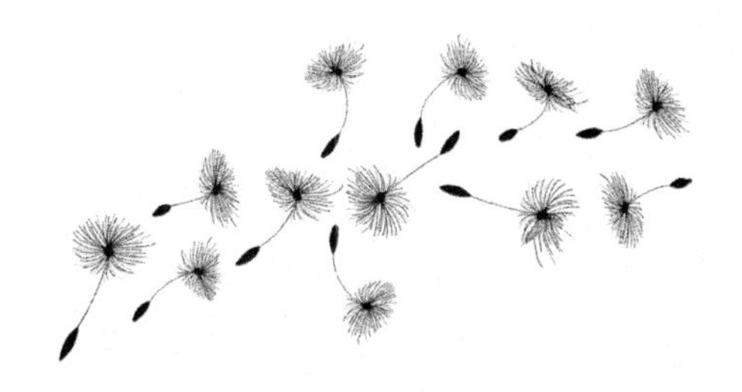

Fairy life is full of troubles,
Bluebell gets in awful muddles,
But with her friends,
She finds a way,
To always save the fairy day.

In this story you will see,
A fluffy little Bumble Bee,
Bees help to make the flowers grow,
And bees buzz happily as they go.

CONTENTS

Bluebell
The Great Honeypot Robbery

P.J. Reed

Chapter One

The Missing Honey

The sun shone through the little window of the red and white spotted toadstool house, hidden in the middle of Therwen Woods. Suddenly, the sunbeams changed into tiny balls of light and danced through the bedroom window, bouncing off the walls, and jumping all over the bed.

Bluebell yawned and waved the dancing balls to one side. She stretched and grinned as the balls of light bounced from her bed and away through her open bedroom door.

Bluebell pulled her soft green mossy

blanket to one side and climbed out of her little conker shell bed.

The bed groaned and then went back to sleep, snoring happily.

Bluebell waved her hand. Instantly, her bright blue pyjamas changed into an even brighter blue dress. The dress was

made from beautiful bluebell petals, which rustled when she moved.

Bluebell walked over to the polished shell mirror that hung on her bedroom wall and brushed her blue hair until it shone so much, little sparks shot out from it.

Outside her bedroom window, a family of blue birds sat and twittered as they waited for their breakfast.

It was going to be a good day.

Bluebell had had a busy week granting wishes to lots of boys and girls. She loved her job, but she also loved her days off too.

Today was one of her rare days off. Bluebell decided to bake some cakes, as fairies love cakes, particularly, honey-flavoured cupcakes. She ran down the toadstool stalk staircase. The staircase opened into a bright, white living room. Tall bookshelves had been carved into the white stalk and filled most of the room.

The floor was covered in rugs of springy, green moss and there were brown shiny pebbles to sit on. In the centre of the room, hidden beneath the twisting stalk staircase, was the kitchen.

Bluebell took her large cream mixing bowl and a wooden spoon from the kitchen cupboard, beneath the acorn shell sink. Then she opened a tiny wooden door in the toadstool wall, to reveal an even smaller room.

The room was lined with shelves filled with hanging dried herbs, tiny glass pots, jam jars, and china jugs. The jars were filled with delicious fairy food such as pickled dandelion leaves, strawberry jelly, and raspberry jam. At the back of the pantry was a glowing jar of marmalade made with magic dust sprinkles, which Bluebell kept for special fairy emergencies.

'Aha, there you are!' Bluebell said as she reached in and tried to grab a bright yellow honeypot.

Two tiny china legs appeared, and the honeypot ran along the shelf. The other jugs and jars on the shelf sprouted arms and began to clap and cheer as the honeypot ran on. Bluebell sighed. Sometimes living in a magical kingdom was very hard work. Bluebell flapped her wings and flew into the cupboard. She caught the honeypot as it jumped down from the shelf and tried to run out of the pantry door.

'Oh no you don't!' Bluebell panted, 'I just want a tiny bit of honey.'

A face and two arms appeared on the honeypot. The arms crossed and the face frowned. This was odd because the honeypot was usually happy to share its honey with her.

Something was wrong.

Bluebell opened the lid of the honeypot

and peered inside. It was almost empty! Bluebell frowned.

She was sure she had filled the honeypot only yesterday. Quickly, Bluebell put the pot back inside the cupboard and shut the door before anything else tried to escape.

'Oh snap!' Bluebell said, 'I have no honey! I can't make honey cakes with no honey! I will have to fly to the Office of Honey in the Honeyfields to get some more honey. Then I will be able to make my cakes.'

Bluebell put the honeypot in her pocket. Then she slipped on her sandals and stood on the front step of her toadstool house. 'I will be back soon,' she called and flapped her beautiful blue wings.

Soon she was flying through Therwen Wood. The sun shone and cast a darker shadow of herself on the path as she flew by. Bluebell flapped her wings faster and whizzed down the path, but she could never beat her shadow.

Shadows were just too quick. Bluebell smiled as she approached the Honeyfields.

The Honeyfields were a group of sweet-smelling flower meadows. Huge golden honeypots stood in the middle of the meadows.

Bluebell watched in delight as she

saw a group of honeybees flying towards the Honeyfields in a ‘V’ shape.

A big bumblebee lifted the lid off a honeypot, while the little honeybees formed a line in front of it and one by one, they flew over the honeypot and carefully poured their golden honey treasure inside. The lead honeybee wriggled his wings from side to side and the rest of the honeybees formed a ‘V’ shape behind him. Then they all raised their black furry legs and saluted the bumblebee.

The bumblebee stood on top of the honeypot and waved to his cousins.

Then the honeybees turned and flew off into the blue sky. The bumblebee watched them fly off. He took out a notepad and tape measure, from underneath his arm, and began to measure the amount of honey in the honeypot.

The bumblebees kept a careful watch over the honey to make sure there was enough honey for everyone in Therwen Wood to share.

Bluebell flew into the Honeyfields and landed next to a huge golden, oval-shaped hive standing on a wooden frame with four wooden legs. Over the doorway was a sign saying, 'The Golden Hive, the Office of Honey, Please knock on the door.'

The legs of the Golden Hive were

carved into the shape of trees, wrapped around with twisting ivy leaves.

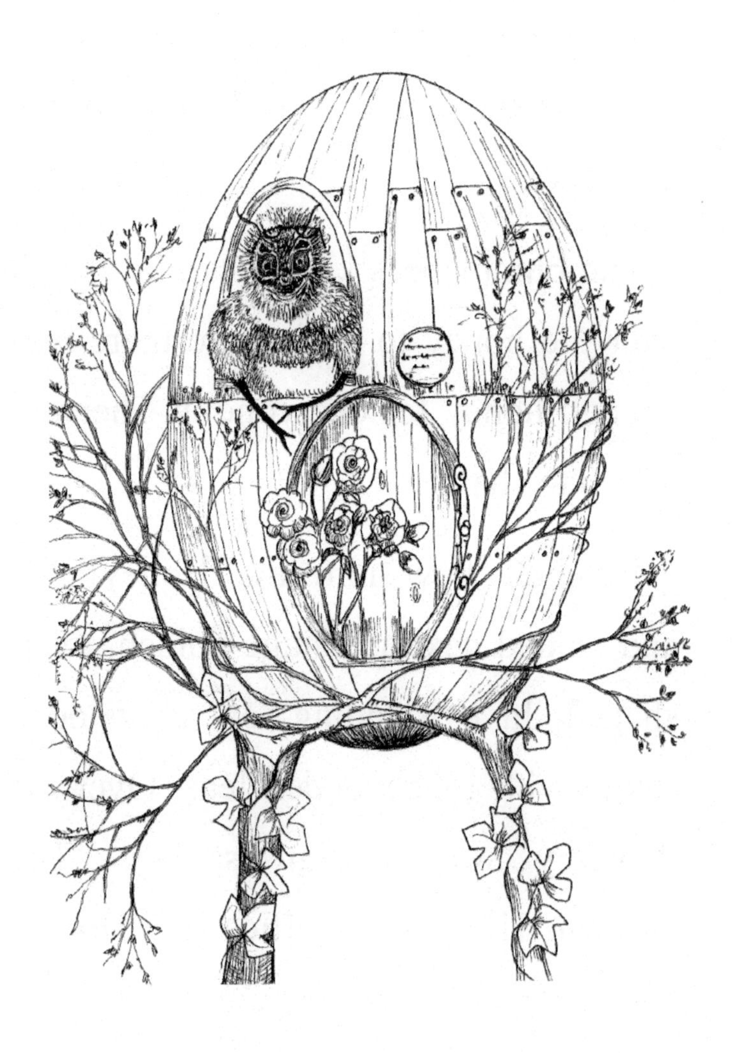

Bluebell knocked on the door of The Golden Hive and waited.

The wooden ivy leaves turned dark green and fluttered in the wind. The leaves knocked against each other like wind chimes, creating a low song which sounded through the tree. A tiny window high up in the hive opened.

'Hello, is anyone there?' a fuzzy black and yellow striped head popped out of the window.

'Hi! It's only me Master Bertie,' called Bluebell.

The bumblebee poked his head further out of the window.

'Be careful Bertie! You are going to

fall out!' said Bluebell in alarm. 'Pull your glasses down, they are on your forehead!'

'Oh!' said the bee. 'I forgot I wasn't wearing them, silly meeee,' he buzzed and pulled them down over his eyes with one furry black leg.

Chapter Two
The Golden Hive

The bee squinted through his round, black-rimmed glasses. Then he smiled.

'Ah, it's Bluebell from the Office of Wishes, isn't it? I recognise your blue hair!'

'Hello! Master Bertie,' said Bluebell as she bowed politely to the bumblebee. 'Please may I have some of your honey?'

'Yes certainly. I will be down in a second,' Bertie replied. The little window closed, and a loud buzzing echoed from inside the hive. 'Stand back,' said Bertie the bumblebee, 'I am opening the door.'

Bluebell looked at the little oval door set into the tree trunk. A beautiful rosebush had been carved into the door. Its thorny stem circled around the door.

There was a clunk and a whir.

The roses burst from the door and a lovely rosy scent filled the air. Then one by one, the thorns covering the door and pinning it to the tree, rolled backwards into the door.

The door swung open, to reveal a rather large bumblebee standing in the doorway. His fluffy black and yellow belly was so big, it almost filled the doorway. He wore a big, furry black and yellow coat, even though it was a very

mild day.

The bee's little wings buzzed. Bertie hovered in the air and landed next to Bluebell. He pushed his reading glasses further along his nose.

Bluebell bowed politely to the bee.

Bertie bowed back, his glasses falling onto the end of his nose. 'Please follow me.'

His tiny wings buzzed up and down.

Bluebell frowned. She did not think such tiny wings would be able to carry such a big bee. The bee's wings buzzed faster and faster. Suddenly, the bee took off and headed straight towards the Honeyfields.

'Wait for me!' Bluebell called as she flew off after the bee.

The Honeyfields were located between Therwen River and the Tinkling Meadows. There were about twenty giant, golden honeypots in the meadow. The honeypots glowed amber in the sunlight. Bertie tapped the side of the nearest honeypot. It sounded hollow.

'This is the one,' Bertie announced. He turned the little tap on the side of the honeypot. Thick drops of delicious, golden honey began to plop slowly into Bluebell's little yellow honeypot.

Five minutes later the honeypot was full. Bertie handed Bluebell the pot. Quickly, she put the lid on the honeypot and gave Bertie three golden pennies. Bertie smiled and put the pennies in his brown drawstring purse.

'Thank you for the honey,' Bluebell said happily.

‘You are very welcome,’ said Master Bertie as he bowed.

Suddenly, the field was filled with the sound of a thousand tiny voices. Bluebell put her head to one side and listened.

The hanging white flowers on the trumpet trees had opened and were sounding out the time across Therwen Wood.

‘Oh my, look at the time!’ Bertie said as he pointed to the nearest trumpet tree.

‘It’s nine o’clock! Queen Caraway is having a big party tonight and we must fly her twenty large pots of honey, so her cooks can make honeycomb hills, honey cakes, and golden cookies.' He said hungrily, and the two black antennae on the top of his head waggled. 'Hopefully, there will be some leftovers too!'

Then he bowed once more and quickly buzzed back to the Office of Honey.

Bluebell smiled. She liked bees; they always had such good manners.

Chapter Three
The Palace Guards

Bluebell flapped her long wings and flew home to make her delicious honey cakes.

Her house was soon filled with the smell of warm honey and cooling cupcakes. Bluebell made herself a cup of nettle tea and picked the biggest cupcake. It was still warm and smelled wonderful.

She sat down at the kitchen table. Then she gasped as she saw the state of the kitchen.

Cream china mixing bowls were stacked one on top of the other in the sink. The sticky cake mixture had plopped down from the bowls onto the polished acorn sink, and someone had put floury white footprints all over her shiny wooden floor. Bluebell grinned.

She unscrewed the tiny acorn from its cup which hung from her silver necklace. Then she tipped a bit of the sparkling magic dust into her hand and blew it across the messy kitchen.

'Fairy magic, please tidy this kitchen for me,' Bluebell said as she wriggled her fingers at the mess. A glittery blue trail of magic shot from her fingertips.

The mixing bowls leapt from the sink and hung in the air, as the taps turned, filling the sink with steamy water. Then the washing-up liquid giggled. Its middle squeezed inwards, and a jet of liquid flew into the air, and landed in the sink.

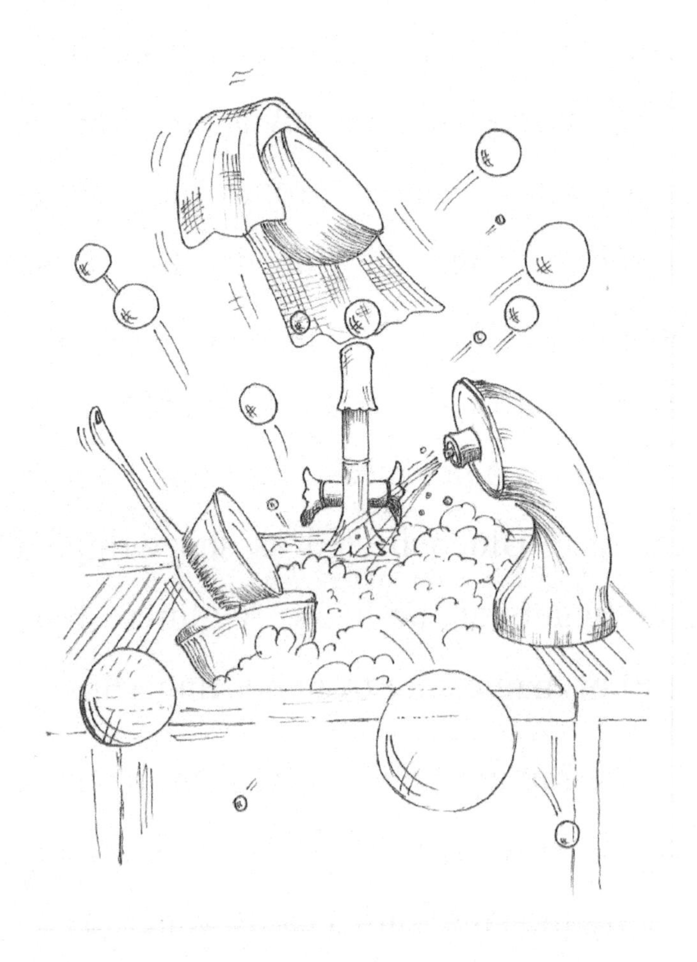

Instantly, the sink filled with rainbow-coloured bubbles. Some of the bubbles rose into the air and whizzed around the kitchen, playing chase with each other.

'Ahem,' Bluebell said as she picked up her cupcake.

Then one by one the mixing bowls dropped into the foamy sink. A tall yellow washing-up brush dived into the sink. Moments later it appeared, its head surrounded in white bubbles, as it began to scrub the first bowl clean.

After a while, the bowl squeaked, and the washing-up brush flipped the bowl into the air. The bowl was caught in mid-air by a red tea towel, who wiped the bowl until it was dry.

A flock of flying wooden clothes pegs swooped down, picked up the bowl, and flew it back to the cupboard, as the next dirty bowl splashed into the sink.

Bluebell grinned.

One of the good things about being a fairy was that she never had to tidy up. She brushed the cake crumbs off her dress. A white pan and brush scurried out from a hole in the toadstool wall. The whiskers on their long noses wrinkled as they scampered across the floor to clean up the crumbs.

Suddenly, there was a loud knock on the door. Bluebell frowned. She shook her head and put the half-eaten cupcake back on its plate.

‘I wonder who it is. They seem in a great hurry for a Saturday morning,’ she said as she walked to the door.

Someone knocked again. They knocked so loudly that the teacups on the shelf jumped and rattled.

‘I’m coming!’ Bluebell called as she flew quickly to the door.

Bluebell landed and opened the front door.

There in the doorway were two huge palace guards. They were both dressed in purple jackets and trousers. On the pocket of their jackets was a picture of the Silver Palace, the great palace in the north of Therwen Wood where Queen Caraway lived. On their heads they wore golden helmets with long nose covers. Metal swords hung from their leather sword belts.

'Er… hello,' Bluebell said looking very confused. 'Can I help you?'

The taller gnome guard looked down at Bluebell and sniffed loudly.

'You smell of honey,' he said.

'Er… yes, I probably do!' Bluebell replied. She blushed and her light blue skin turned bright purple. 'Um… I have just eaten a honey cupcake. I have nine left over, if you would like one?' she offered politely.

The wider gnome guard with a white, neatly plaited white beard shook his head.

'We are here on official palace business, Miss fairy. We are not allowed to eat cupcakes on duty.'

'You were seen flying towards the Honeyfields today. What you were doing there?' asked the taller guard.

'Of course,' said Bluebell, 'I needed some more honey. I ran out and I wanted to make some honey cakes, so I flew to the Honeyfields to get some more.'

'I see,' the guards said as they nodded at each other. 'So… you admit that you stole the honey. You had better come back to the palace with us!'

'But I did not steal anything!' said Bluebell. 'I bought some honey from Master Bertie! Just go and ask him!'

'We would but he was attacked while checking the Golden Hives and left hanging in mid-air fast asleep and no one can wake him up! He has been taken to the Mushroom of Magical

Diseases. Hopefully, the nurse fairies there will be able to cure him.'

'Oh no, poor Master Bertie,' Bluebell said. 'I hope he wakes up soon.'

Then the guards nodded at each other. They grabbed Bluebell by her elbows and marched her off to the palace.

Chapter Four
The Silver Palace

The Silver Palace was a beautiful shining palace on the northern edge of Therwen Wood. It was the home of Queen Caraway, the elder sister of Queen Winterberry.

The Silver Palace was surrounded by tall silver birch trees. Their trunks were silvery white and, here and there, the bark had peeled off to reveal slashes of dark grey. Their delicate branches were filled with shining green, heart-shaped leaves.

As the guard cart approached the palace, the silver birches waved their branches and a handful of leaves fell down onto the cart. The little grey rabbits pulling the cart wrinkled their noses up and sniffed the leaves as they fell. Then they grabbed a bunch of

leaves to nibble as they hopped towards the palace.

Bluebell peered out from the bars of the cart and gasped as she saw the four white towers of the Silver Palace towering above the clouds. On the top of each tower was a long, thin flag with a picture of a white hill. Pink roses and green ivy grew up the walls of the castle and gave the castle a beautiful smell of roses.

The castle was surrounded by a sea blue lake. The top of the lake rippled white as kelpies cantered through the water. Their green and blue manes sparkled in the sunlight. They tossed their heads and neighed as the cart approached the drawbridge.

The gnome guards shouted up to the castle and a wooden bridge lowered. The guards marched Bluebell across the bridge. Below them, Bluebell could see some merpeople sitting on the bottom of the lake and watching them.

The merpeople whispered to each other, their words forming white bubbles in the water. The bubbles popped open as they reached the surface of the lake and Bluebell could hear the whispers of the merpeople. They were saying that she was a bad fairy, who had been caught stealing, and that she was a thief.

It made her very sad, and Bluebell bit

her lip to stop herself from crying.

The guard cart stopped at a white wooden door, the entrance into the Queen's palace. The tall guard knocked on the door and it swung open. A mouse in a black dinner jacket and silver bowtie ran up to greet Bluebell.

'Hello and welcome to the Silver Palace. My name is Eric Wanderfield, I am the Head Butler here. Would you like a cup of tea?' he asked bowing to Bluebell.

Bluebell bowed back to Eric and was about to reply, but the tall gnome guard shook his head.

'We are here on official palace business. There is no time for tea,' he said gruffly and pushed Bluebell along the hallway to the Queen's Hall.

'Well, really, gnomes are so rude!' Eric said shaking his head. 'There is always time for a cup of tea. I will put the kettle on just in case,' and he ran on all fours to the kitchen.

The Queen's Hall was beautiful. The hall was made from silver birches, carved into the shape of columns, their branches twisting up into the ceiling. The ceiling had been painted midnight blue and sprinkled with silver stars. While the windows were made of diamond shaped pieces of glass which sparkled in the sun and covered the floor in tiny blue, red, and yellow lights.

A row of royal guards stood each side of the hall dressed in red coats, white shirts, and red stripy trousers. Each guard held a long stick of white oak which shimmered with magic dust.

At the end of the hall, were some white steps. At the top of the steps was a large throne carved into the shape of a rose.

The throne was surrounded by white pots containing lots of little green plant shoots. When the plants were big enough the Queen's guards planted them around the wood, so Therwen Wood was always filled with beautiful, sweet-smelling flowers.

In the centre of the throne, sat the

Queen. She was wearing a huge white gown.

The guards walked over to the Queen, and they all bowed. The Queen looked at Bluebell and pointed a long, white finger at her.

'Did she take my honey?' the Queen demanded.

Bluebell went bright purple and shook her head so hard the bells on her shoes jingled.

Gunnar, an elderly court gnome in a stiff black coat and matching black trousers, stepped out from behind the throne. His beard was so long that it reached down to his waist. He cleared his throat and read from a piece of paper.

'Your Majesty, may I present to you, Bluebell, a wish fairy originally from Flower Meadows. She has been charged with stealing your missing honey. She was seen flying towards the Honeyfields. Later, fresh honey cakes could be smelt through the window of her toadstool home,' Gunnar said as he bowed to the Queen.

Bluebell shook her head and glared at the court gnome. 'I would never steal anything, it's wrong and fairies will always try to do what is right and good!'

'That is true, fairies do not steal anything, especially not from their Queen,' Gunnar nodded.

Queen Caraway frowned. She took a handful of berries from the berry bowl by her throne and gobbled them all up.

'Hmm...,' said Queen Caraway, wiping the berry juice from her face with the sleeve of her dress. 'Well Gunnar, are you quite sure she's a fairy then. Perhaps she is an imp? They are always up to no good!'

'Hmm…,' replied Gunnar. He took a pair of glasses from his jacket pocket and placed them on the end of his pointed nose. He looked carefully at Bluebell.

'The suspect appears to be blue. Imps are generally grey, with grey wings. Therefore, I believe she is indeed a fairy.'

The Queen looked from Bluebell to the gnome standing next to her, 'I see. It's decided then.'

Bluebell gasped and looked at the Queen.

'You are indeed a fairy,' said the Queen.

‘Well done, your Majesty, a very wise decision,’ Gunnar said bowing.

‘So, where is the evidence for the theft? Just where are the honey cakes this fairy made?’ the Queen demanded.

‘Here they are, Ma’am,’ said Gunnar. He wriggled his fingers and the air filled with sparkling dust. Then a plateful of warm honey cakes appeared in his hand.

The Queen’s face lit up. She grabbed a honey cake and started munching it, the crumbs falling down the front of her white dress.

Bluebell stared at the Queen as she began to lick the sticky honey from her fingers.

‘Begging your pardon, your Majesty,’

said Bluebell bowing to the Queen, 'but I did not steal any honey.'

The Queen stopped eating and stared at Bluebell. Her eyes narrowed.

Bluebell knew that the Queen did not believe her, and she felt very sad.

Suddenly, the hall door slammed open and the sound of running feet echoed through the hallway. Everyone turned around to see what was happening.

Billy, the junior bumblebee, ran into the hall, a very large book in his hand. His glasses fell from his nose. As he reached to save them, he dropped the book on the floor. Without his glasses, he could not see the book. He tripped over it and skidded across the floor on his round furry tummy, crashing into a statue of the Queen.

The statue wobbled and leaned over.

Everybody in the hall gasped in horror as they watched the statue slowly fall and crash to the ground, shattering into tiny white pieces.

Bluebell side-stepped her guards and ran to help Billy. She found his glasses among the pieces of statue. Bluebell wiped them on her dress and handed them back to him.

'Here you are Billy, are you alright?' she asked.

Billy buzzed unhappily.

'Yes, I'm fine but the statue isn't!' he said.

The Queen shouted at Billy. 'How dare you break my statue… and who are you anyway?'

Billy cleared his throat and his buzzing got louder. He bowed to the Queen.

'I am Billy Bumblebee, the junior bumblebee at the Office of Honey. I heard Bluebell had been arrested so I flew here straight away. Bluebell bought one potful of honey from Master Bertie this morning. Here it is written in the Honey Money Book.'

Billy handed the big book to Gunnar. The old gnome flicked through the pages and nodded.

'Your Majesty, the book says that

Bluebell did indeed buy one potful of honey this morning. Therefore, she did not steal the honey!'

The book slammed itself shut, grew wings and flew back to Billy. Billy caught the book and tucked it safely under his arm.

'Well,' demanded the Queen, 'Just who did steal my honey then?'

Chapter Five
The Honey Thief

The great hall went silent. The guards stood in rows and stared at the paintings on the wall. Billy took his glasses off and began to polish them with the white hanky he kept hidden in his pocket.

The Queen stood up and put her hands on her hips and shouted, 'Someone has stolen my honey. I wish to know who it is!'

The castle walls began to glow amber.

A wish had been said. Suddenly, a wish gnome appeared.

Bluebell groaned.

It was the grumpy gnome from the

Office of Wishes. The gnome bowed to the Queen and the bell on the top of his floppy white hat jingled. The gnome bowed and then smiled at the Queen.

Bluebell was shocked. She had never seen a gnome be so polite before.

'Master Tobin, at your service, your Majesty,' said the gnome. 'We take wishes very seriously at the Office of Wishes. All the wish fairies are out working today in the human world today. It has been a very busy time, but as soon as one becomes available…'

'I want a wish fairy… now!' shouted the Queen.

Master Tobin began to sweat under his white jacket. 'I'm very sorry, your

Majesty. I will find one as soon as possible.'

'Guards take him to the tower!' the Queen said pointing at the shaking gnome. The two guards picked up the shaking gnome and began to drag him from the hall.

'Wait!' said Bluebell stepping forward. 'I can help. I am a wish fairy.'

'Stop!' said the Queen. 'Is she a wish fairy?' she asked pointing at Bluebell.

The guards put the wish gnome down. Master Tobin took his glasses off and polished them carefully. Then he replaced them and stared at Bluebell.

'Bluebell is that you? What are you doing here?' he asked.

The Queen growled and Master Tobin took a couple of steps backwards.

'Er… yes, Bluebell is indeed a wish fairy and a very good wish fairy too. I'm sure she can help you, your Majesty,' he said bowing even lower to the Queen.

'Very well,' said the Queen. 'You must find my missing honey immediately or you will both be taken to the tower!'

Everyone in the hall gasped and turned towards Bluebell.

'Yes, your Majesty. I will find your honey,' Bluebell said. Her face went pale blue, and her legs began to shake as butterfly worries fluttered in her tummy.

Suddenly, the clock on the wall began to whir. A door on the clockface opened and a little man appeared. He bowed to the Queen and then pulled the silver bell two times. He bowed again and went back inside the clock and the door shut behind then.

'It that the time already?' The Queen said. 'My guests will be arriving, and I haven't had my afternoon nap yet. She stood up and hurried from the hall. Everyone bowed as she left.

Billy buzzed over to Bluebell. 'So, just how are you going to find the honey thief then?'

'Hmm…,' said Bluebell. 'I am not sure, but I am a wish fairy, and a wish has been granted. I will have to find the missing honey. I think I need to go back and look at the Golden Hive for clues. Would you like to come with me?'

'Yes, please! If we can find out who stole the honey perhaps, we can find a cure and break the spell on poor Uncle Bertie!' Billy Bumblebee buzzed.

Someone coughed loudly.

Bluebell and Billy turned round to see Master Tobin scratching his pointed ear with his quill pen. 'I will accompany you too. You may need help from a big, strong gnome if you find the ruffian who attacked poor Master Bertie.'

'Yesss,' buzzed Billy. 'If only we could find a big strong gnome!'

Master Tobin went bright red and began to wag his finger in the direction of the cheeky bumblebee. Billy giggled and buzzed flying backwards away from the gnome.

'Watch out!' screamed Bluebell, but it was too late.

Billy flew straight into the flowerpots by the throne. The flowerpots knocked into each other. The large flowerpot at the top of the steps fell over and began to roll down the steps. A trail of brown soil followed the pot. The pot plopped off the last step and smashed onto the floor.

Mud, china, and broken bits of leaf, scattered across the white floor.

‘Oh no!’ cried Bluebell as she stared at the mess in horror.

‘Oh snap!’ buzzed Billy, as his worried, furry face appeared in between some fern leaves.

‘Bother that bee!’ exclaimed Master Tobin. ‘We had better clean that mess up before the Queen finds out, or we will all be locked in the tower!’ He bent down to pick up a sad looking leaf.

Suddenly, a little mouse in a smart white apron scurried out of a hole in the palace wall, just behind a huge statue of the Queen. She was holding a dustpan and brush.

‘Hello, my dears, I’m Mrs Peep,’ said the mouse bowing.

Quickly, the mouse swept up the mess and ran over to a huge china pot beside the royal rose throne.

The pot was round with a flat bottom which stopped it rolling away across the floor. It was decorated with pictures of magical creatures from the mountains just beyond Therwen Wood.

There were fire-breathing dragons with shiny red bellies and strange looking birds with long golden tails, all flying above the snow-covered mountains. A stream ran from the top of the mountain filling up the lake at the foot of the mountain.

Suddenly, the lake began to sparkle. A little white cloud flew out from the lake and hovered just above the pot.

'Stand back, my dears!' ordered Mrs Peep. 'It's going to rain!'

The cloud grew bigger and bigger until it filled the whole hall. Then it started to rain, washing the last remains of mud from the tiles until the floor gleamed white once more.

'Thank you so much for your help,' said Bluebell, as Tobin and Billy bowed to the mouse.

'Oh, you are most welcome, my dears, anyway the pot did most of the work. It's such a good tidying pot,' she said as she stroked its sides. The pot jumped happily from side to side.

'Well, I must go home. I've got the babies to feed,' Mrs Peep bowed and ran back to the hole in the wall.

Bluebell grabbed Tobin and Billy by the arms. 'Right, let's get out of here before anything else happens! I will use my emergency magic dust and fly us to the Honeyfields. We will go to the Golden Hive first as that was where poor Bertie was attacked.'

Bluebell unscrewed her silver acorn and tipped the remaining dust into her hand. Then she threw the dust into the air, so it covered the three of them in shining glitter.

'Fairy magic please take us to the Honeyfields.'

The glitter shimmered around them, and they vanished.

Chapter Six
Footprints

Bluebell, Billy Bumblebee, and Tobin landed in a sparkle of magic dust, just in front of the Golden Hive.

Master Tobin swayed as he landed and fell on his bottom. His pink face looked rather white.

'Are you alright, Master Tobin?' Bluebell asked, running over to help him up.

'Gnomes are not meant to disappear in clouds of magic dust. We are more of the two feet on the ground at all times type of people,' Tobin announced. He pulled his hat down firmly on his head and the silver bell at the end jingled.

'You look like you are going to be sick!' joked Billy. He flapped his wings and turned a circle in the air. 'I do not understand gnomes. Flying is the best way to travel.' He stopped flapping his wings and landed next to Bluebell, safely out of the reach of the angry-looking gnome.

'Oh! bother that bee,' grumbled the gnome. 'Well, let's just get on with it, shall we?'

'Get on with what may I ask?' a deep voice behind them said.

They spun round.

In front of them was a woodland stoat guard dressed in a green coat, a white shirt, and a pair of green stripy trousers.

‘Er… hello,’ said Bluebell as they bowed to the guard.

‘Are you all here to steal more honey?’ asked the guard, standing up on his two back legs and glaring down at them.

‘Of course not!’ replied Master Tobin crossly. ‘A gnome never steals.’

Bluebell shot Tobin a look, warning him to be quiet.

‘No master guard,’ she bowed again,

‘We are here on orders from the Queen, to find out who stole her honey.’

'Hmm…' said the stoat guard, scratching the white whiskers on his face with his paw. 'So, the Queen sent you?

‘Yes,’ the three of them nodded.

‘To find out who stole the honey?’ asked the stoat guard as his long brown tail flicked from side to side. ‘I see, so the woodland guards don’t have to. We have been trying to find the thieves but have not found a single clue and nobody wants to tell the Queen that!’

Bluebell shook her head. ‘Well, the Queen ordered us to find the honey thieves, but we would be very grateful for any help.’ She smiled at the guard.

‘I see,’ said the guard. He took off his green hat and mopped the sweat from his face. ‘Of course, the Woodland Guard will be happy to help you. Here are the keys to all the Golden

Honeypots. Please lock the doors when you are finished.' Then the guard fell forward onto his four legs and scampered away to the woods.

'Well, he was rather quick to get away,' buzzed Billy, his black antennae moving in all directions on the top of his head.

Bluebell laughed. 'I'm not surprised. I don't think I would want to tell the Queen that we couldn't find any clues either!'

'Hmm…' said Tobin, stroking his long white beard. That is very true. We need to find a clue before the Queen summons us back to the Palace.'

'Yesss…' buzzed Billy, 'but what do clues actually look like?'

Bluebell thought for a moment. 'I think a clue is something that just doesn't look right.'

'I see,' said Billy, 'like a carrot growing in an apple tree.'

'Exactly,' laughed Bluebell.

'But there are no apple trees here. The apple trees are at Pippin Orchards, almost a mile away.' Tobin said shaking his head. 'I don't think they will have many carrot clues there either. I was there only yesterday with Mrs Tobin, picking apples for her delicious apple pie and there were definitely no carrots growing in the apple trees.' Tobin said putting his hands on his hips and nodding to himself.

'Er… a clue doesn't have to look like a carrot, Tobin, it's just something that looks wrong.'

The trumpet trees blasted three times.

'Oh snap! Listen to the time! It's getting late now. The Queen will soon be awake,' Bluebell said. 'We need to get going and find a clue quickly!'

'Right,' said Billy, and he flew at top speed around the field dodging in and out of the giant honeypots.

'Bother that bee! He will never find any clues. We need to do this slowly and carefully. You look inside the Office of Honey.' Tobin said as he handed the keys to Bluebell. 'I will walk around the other honeypots.' He nodded and walked into the meadow; his black eyes fixed on the grasses swaying around the bottom of the honeypots.

'Right!' said Bluebell to herself. 'I will need to check the office for clues. I just hope the honey thief doesn't come back!'

Chapter Seven
The Golden Hive

Bluebell looked at the little oval door set into the tree trunk and put the key in the keyhole. There was a clunk and a whir as wooden roses burst from the door. The thorns covering the door and pinning it to the tree, rolled backwards into the door.

The door swung open.

Cautiously, Bluebell walked inside the Golden Hive. The wall of the first floor of the hive was covered in hexagonal shaped wooden boxes. The boxes were filled with pieces of paper and old looking books. Bluebell picked up one of the books. It was a heavy book with a picture of fluffy pink clover on its front. Bluebell opened the book.

The white pages began to bulge as a paper clover plant grew out from the pages of the book. Two green stems grew upwards and swayed as three round leaves burst onto the end of each stem. Slowly, the flower stalk grew taller and opened into a beautiful purple clover flower ball.

The smell of vanilla ice cream filled the air. Yellow words written in Bertie's neat bee handwriting appeared on the page. It read, 'Clover flowers make very good food for young bees.' Then, a little packet of clover seeds appeared on the page. The packet of seeds sprouted wings and flew through the open door of the Golden Hive.

Quickly, Bluebell shut the book. She did not want the whole of Therwen Woods covered in clover flowers, no matter how nicely they smelled. She was sure the Queen would not be happy about it.

Carefully, Bluebell put the book back in its box, before any other seeds could escape. She looked around the hive, puffed out her cheeks, and blew the hair from her eyes. Finding clues was a lot harder than she thought.

Suddenly, a breeze ruffled some of the papers. One of the papers floated from the box and fell on the floor in front of her. Bluebell shivered in the cold wind. Then she smiled. There was no wind inside the hive and yet there was. This was very odd and needed to be investigated.

A little spiral staircase circled around the walls of the hive. Bluebell grinned and began to climb the staircase. The stairs went past the boxes at the top of the Golden Hive. Some of the boxes were windows and glowed yellow with warm sunlight. Other boxes were paintings of flowers, trees, and bees.

The flowers turned their heads as Bluebell walked by and smiled. Bluebell stopped by a painting of a tall, horse chestnut tree, filled with copper conkers, and big green leaves.

'Excuse me, Master Tree,' said Bluebell. 'I am looking for clues. Have you noticed anything odd happening here?'

There was a whooshing sound as the branches of the tree began to move. Some of the conkers plopped into the bottom of the painting. Its leaves turned brown and began to fall from the swaying branches. However, instead of falling to the ground, the leaves burst from the painting and swirled upwards towards the top of the staircase.

Bluebell felt the wind from the painting pushing her up the stairs. 'Do you want me to follow the leaves?' she asked.

A wrinkled brown face appeared on the trunk of the chestnut tree. The face nodded at Bluebell.

'I see,' said Bluebell. 'Thank you so much for your help!'

She followed the trail of dancing leaves.

The leaves led to a tiny wooden box window at the top of the Hive. The sun shone through the window, and something sparkled on the stairs below. The leaves swirled around her legs and then disappeared down the stairs, heading back to their painting. Bluebell looked at the stairs and gasped. The step was covered in broken bubble glass. Someone had smashed the window.

Unlike human glass, magic glass was made from stretched bubbles. When bubble glass broke it burst into lots of tiny bubbles. Bluebell watched as the sun shone through the window. A trail of bubbles in the shape of shoeprints led from the window down the stairs.

Bluebell gasped.

Someone must have broken the window and snuck down to the bottom of the Office of Honey, to steal the key to open all the honeypots. Poor Bertie Bee must have got in the thief's way and been put to sleep, so that the thief could steal his key.

Bluebell's wing curled over and scratched her head as she thought carefully about the clues.

To get to the window the thief had to either climb very well or have wings and fly. A spider could climb up to the top of the Office of Honey easily but then Bluebell had never seen a spider wearing shoes. The thief had to be someone who could fly and who wore shoes. It was all very confusing, as Bluebell knew many people in Therwen Wood who did both.

Then Bluebell grinned. She borrowed a piece of paper from the nearby hexagonal box and placed it on one of the shoeprints. The bubbles made a rainbow-coloured print of the shoe on the paper. It was the shoeprint of the thief. Now all she had to do was find the person who matched the footprint.

It was her first big clue, and she ran back down the stairs to tell Billy and Tobin.

Chapter Eight

The Missing Honey

Bluebell flew out of the Office of Honey and carefully locked the front door. She could not see Master Tobin or Billy Bumblebee anywhere.

'They must still be looking for clues in the Honeyfields,' she said to a passing robin. The bird nodded in agreement and flew off to find its friends.

Bluebell flew towards the honeypots. She bowed as a honeybee carrying a tiny pot of honey in its little black legs buzzed passed her on its way to refill the giant honeypots. The delicious smell of sweet honey hung over the field.

Bluebell looked at the row of honeypots and gasped.

There was a gap in the neat rows of honey pots. One of the honeypots was missing. She landed in the space where the honeypot had been.

'Don't step on it!' Tobin shouted.

'Step on what?' asked Bluebell, her left foot still hanging in the air, as she landed in the yellow circle where the missing honeypot had been.

Tobin hurried forward and picked up a piece of sparkling grey cloth.

'What's that?' Bluebell asked staring at the piece of cloth.

'I think it was ripped off the thief's jacket when he lifted the honeypot,' Tobin said, stroking his long white beard thoughtfully. He smelt the cloth and nodded. 'It smells of honey.'

'I see that's a great clue Master Tobin, well done! I found a clue too! I got this in the Office of Honey,' said Bluebell as she showed Tobin the picture of the shoeprint she had found. They placed the picture on the ground and put their feet next to it. Tobin's foot was almost twice as wide as the shoeprint.

'Hmm…,' said Tobin blushing red. 'The thief is definitely not a gnome then. Its feet are just too small and narrow. Us gnomes have good big feet because we do so much walking, you see.'

'I think your feet are very sensibly sized,' Bluebell said as she smiled at the gnome.

Billy buzzed over and landed next to Tobin.

'And where have you been?' asked the gnome crossly. 'Playing 'fly and catch' with those silly cousins of yours, no doubt.'

'Well… I…' Billy buzzed. He had indeed spent most of the afternoon playing with his cousins and had forgotten to look for any clues. He looked very sad.

'Oh… don't worry, Billy,' said Bluebell. 'We have found some important clues. The thief's feet are slightly bigger than a fairy but not as big as a gnome.'

'And...' said Tobin happily. 'The thief was wearing a grey shirt when he stole the honeypot.'

'Hmm…' said Billy as he wriggled his feelers towards the gnome and grinned. 'So, we are looking for someone slightly bigger than a fairy, wearing a ripped grey shirt, who can lift a whole honeypot, and fly it through Therwen Wood without anyone noticing. So, who is it?'

'Well,' said the gnome crossly, 'we haven't figured that part out just yet!'

There was a rumbling sound.

Billy and Tobin both looked at Bluebell. The poor fairy had gone dark blue.

'I'm so sorry,' Bluebell said, clutching her tummy, 'It's just that I haven't eaten since breakfast!'

'Oh dear!' said Tobin shaking his head from side to side so that the bell on the end of his hat rang. 'That's no good at all.'

There was another rumbling noise as Tobin looked down at his round stomach in horror. Billy laughed so much that he buzzed into the air and did a backflip as he held his giggling, furry black tummy.

Then, as if by magic, a woodland guard appeared. The guard scampered towards them on four little white legs carrying a picnic basket in its mouth.

‘I think we are in for a treat!’ Tobin smiled and rubbed his tummy.

'Good afternoon, thief catchers, we had a report at the station down by the riverbank that you have had no lunch. Please accept this as a thank you from the woodland guards.' The stoat placed the basket on the floor, stood on his hind legs, and saluted the three thief finders. Then he went back down on his four brown and white furry legs and hurried back across the fields.

Tobin knelt and opened the little picnic basket. The smell of fresh strawberries and apples floated on the air. The gnome took a red and white chequered tablecloth from the basket and laid it over the grass.

Bluebell and Billy sat on the cloth and

watched as Tobin pulled out a large cake stand filled with delicious looking cupcakes. Next, he pulled out a plate of freshly made scones with little pots of strawberry jam and thick fresh cream.

The scones were so light they began to float off the plate. Quickly, Bluebell and Billy grabbed a scone each as they floated by. Tobin handed them a white, china plate and poured everyone a glass of fizzy strawberry juice.

'Ah… this is the life,' said Billy happily wiping the honey cupcake crumbs from his tummy.

'Yes,' replied Bluebell, her mouth covered in chocolate as she took another bite from her gooey chocolate cupcake.

'I didn't realise that being a thief finder would be so filling,' replied Tobin as he lay back on the tablecloth, his hands resting on his tummy as he fell fast asleep.

Chapter Nine
Ice

Bluebell woke with a start. The strawberry scone, that had been resting in her hand, rolled away into the grass. She yawned and sat up. Tobin and Billy were fast asleep, curled up in little snoring balls.

The sun had dropped lower in the sky and grey shadows fell from the honeypots. The trumpet trees sounded five times.

'Oh snap!' said Bluebell. 'We have slept for too long! The Queen's tea party will be starting soon, and we still have not found the missing honey. I hope they have enough honey left for her honey cakes or everyone in the palace will be sent to the tower!'

The leaves on the trumpet trees began to rustle. Bluebell shivered as a cold wind ran through the Honeyfields. The tops of the trees sparkled and turned white with frost. The honeypots glistened as the honey dripped from their taps and turned to ice.

Bluebell shivered and wrapped her wings around her.

'Glacia is that you?' she called, looking up into the sky for the ice fairy. Bluebell frowned. In the summertime, when the sun was high in the sky,

Glacia did not work in the meadows but stayed in the mountains, making sure their tops were always covered with white snow.

Bluebell put her head to one side and listened for Glacia but she could not hear the jingling silver bells on the white boots of the ice fairy at all.

Then, she heard the sound of heavy wing beats in the sky. Bluebell ducked down and crawled over to Billy.

'Wake up Billy. Something is wrong,' she whispered, tugging at his wings. Billy buzzed quietly under his breath and rolled onto his back. Bluebell frowned and pulled his wings again. The bee remained fast asleep.

Bluebell crawled over to Tobin and gently prodded his stomach. The gnome stopped snoring, opened one black eye, and then fell fast asleep again.

'Oh snap!' thought Bluebell. There was magic in the air. She could feel it. Poor Billy and Tobin must have been put under a magical sleeping spell.

The magic acorn hanging on her necklace still had some magic dust left in it. She could use it to try to break the spell and wake them up. However, she was only trained to paint rainbows and to grant wishes. Painting rainbows had gone very wrong. While the one wish she had granted had terrified the little boy when a real live, fire-breathing

dragon had appeared in his bedroom.

'What happens if I cast a spell and accidentally turn them into frogs or something?' Bluebell thought frowning. She really did not want another telling off from Madame Primrose, the rather grumpy Fairy Teacher.

A grey shadow flew across the meadow grass. Bluebell looked up at the sky. A grey imp was flying in and out of the clouds and tucked under his arms were two yellow honeypots. The imp was stealing honey. She had found the honey thief.

Bluebell looked at the sleeping bumblebee and gnome. She shook her head. Bluebell did not have time to wake them up. She leapt into the air and flapped her wings soaring high into the sky after the imp.

The two honeypots had made the imp rather slow, and Bluebell easily caught up with him.

'Those jars are the property of Queen Caraway,' Bluebell shouted at the imp, more bravely than she felt.

'Well... they are now property of Lord Grendel,' the imp replied.

'Put them back where you found them or else!' shouted Bluebell.

'Or else what?' laughed the imp. 'You are a blue fairy, not even part of the woodland guard. What are you going to do... paint a pretty rainbow or something?'

Bluebell's eyes shone a shade bluer, and she grinned.

'I might just do that!' she said. She unscrewed the magic acorn and sprinkled the sparkling magic dust all over her hands.

'W...what are you doing to do?' the

imp said in alarm.

Bluebell smiled. She wriggled her fingers in the air, creating glitter circles. Then she pointed towards the imp. A blue glitter arrow raced through the air towards the imp.

The imp screamed and dropped both honeypots as he tried to escape into the clouds.

He was too late. The fairy spell hit him in the chest, and he somersaulted backwards. The imp screamed and looked down at his chest. Beams of brightly coloured light were exploding from his chest. His whole body was turning into shades of rainbow.

His hair turned red, his face yellow, his hands and feet green, and his grey wings went orange. Then the rainbow colours began to melt, dripping onto the nearby clouds, as his body turned a dark shade of blue. The imp tried to flap his wings and fly away but the wet paint made them too heavy. He hung in the air, crossed his arms, and glared at Bluebell.

'Oh snap!' Bluebell said looking at the blue imp. 'I still can't paint proper rainbows!'

There was a buzzing next to her as Billy appeared carrying the honeypots.

'Thanks for waking us up with the magic dust, it was very clever of you!'

Billy grinned.

'Er… that's ok!' said Bluebell. She looked down between her feet at the Honeyfields below. They were covered in magic dust and twinkling rainbow colours.

Tobin stood by the Golden Hive, his white and red gnome uniform covered in rainbow stripes.

'Oh, double snap!' said Bluebell, as she looked down at the confused multi-coloured gnome.

Chapter Ten
Madame Primrose

There was a whoosh as a sudden wind whirled around the sky. Then the clouds moved to one side to reveal Madame Primrose, Silvertoes, and Marigold, whizzing through the sky at top speed. Madame Primrose raised her hand and the three-fairy patrol stopped and hovered in the air.

‘You are under arrest by order of Queen Caraway for stealing pots of honey. You must come with us to the Silver Palace,’ Madame Primrose said reading from a paper scroll. She stared at the imp from over the top of her reading glasses.

The imp tried to flap his wings and escape, but they will still too wet and heavy to move. ‘Bother that fairy!’ he shouted pointing at Bluebell.

Bluebell’s face turned bright blue and her wings fluttered, covering the imp in blue sparkles which stick to his now blue wings.

‘Argh! Get her away from me!’ the imp shouted. ‘She is a menace!’

Madame Primrose nodded to Silvertoes, who tossed her silvery hair to one side and wriggled her fingers at the imp. A stream of icy glitter shot from her hands towards the imp. The imp put his hands up to cover his face. Immediately, his hands were hit by the stream of ice and stuck together.

Silvertoes flew over and held the wriggling imp by his shoulders.

'Quick Marigold,' said Madame Primrose, 'use your magic.'

Marigold nodded; her long orange hair tipped with yellow, glowing in the sunlight. Her dress was made from lots of long marigold flower petals all sewn together to form a simple top and a huge fluffy orange skirt. She took out a little orange bell from her skirt petals and rang it. The soft flower music was so gentle it made the imp feel very sleepy. He stopped struggling and his grey eyes turned orange.

‘Quick, let’s get him to the palace before he wakes up!’ ordered Madame Primrose.

Marigold and Silvertoes nodded and took hold of the sleeping imp’s arms.

‘Well done, Bluebell,’ smiled Madame Primrose.

‘Er… you’re very welcome,’ said Bluebell in surprise.

‘It was very clever of you to use your special rainbow magic to colour all the clouds with the wrong colours,’ Madame Primrose laughed. ‘How did you know I would be watching?’

‘Er… well, I knew the rainbow patrol

would spot it. They did last time!' Bluebell blushed.

'That is very true,' said Madame Primrose, 'and now the thief has been caught you can start cleaning the clouds.' She checked another scroll attached to her waist by a strand of silk. 'Hmm… today it is meant to be slightly cloudy. So, the clouds need to be painted grey and white.'

Bluebell bowed to her teacher.

'Right then girls, let's be off,' said Madame Primrose.

Silvertoes and Marigold flapped their wings once and tore across the sky, leaving Madame Primrose in a cloud of magic dust.

‘Bother those fairies!’ Madame Primrose said. ‘Why can’t they ever take their time?’

Madame Primrose nodded to Bluebell and quickly flew after Silvertoes, Marigold, and the imp.

Chapter Eleven
The Clouds

'Oh snap!' said Bluebell as she waved goodbye to the fairies and flew back to the Golden Hive. Splashes of blue were beginning to fall from the sky and cover the green meadow grass.

'Well done for catching that imp,' Tobin yawned as he stood next to Bluebell. 'But did you have to turn everything blue?' He said looking up at the dripping sky. 'But at least my new white shirt is still clean,' he said as he took off his rainbow striped, white jacket.

'Er… I'm so sorry,' said Bluebell. 'Everything I touch seems to turn blue.'

'Wee…' giggled Billy Bee as he did a somersault in the air. He landed next to Bluebell and Tobin and shook himself. Drips of blue paint flew from his yellow and black fur.

'Oh no!' Tobin screamed as the blue spots fell all over his clean white shirt.

'Whoops!' Billy grinned at the multicoloured gnome. Then he turned to Bluebell, 'Don't worry Bluebell. We can help you tidy this mess up in no time.'

'Speak for yourself bee!' replied Tobin as he desperately tried to wipe the blue spots from his shirt with his white hanky. ‘There’s no way I can get my bucket and sponge up there.’ The gnome stared at the blue clouds crossing the rainbow-coloured sky.

‘Hmm…’ said Billy, ‘we will see about that. Hop onto my back.’

‘What!’ said the gnome. ‘A gnome never has more than one foot off the ground at a time.’

‘But don’t you want to help Bluebell?’ Billy asked, twirling the black feelers round on his head.

‘Of course, I do!’ said the gnome gruffly.

‘Well hop on board then,’ said Billy.

‘Oh, very well. Just don’t tell the missus,’ Tobin muttered as he leapt on Billy’s back clutching his mop and bucket.

Bluebell whizzed after them.

‘Perhaps I can try to use my magic to get the colour from the sky,’ she said. Bluebell wriggled her fingers and screwed up her nose in concentration.

A trail of glitter flew across the sky and the clouds turned bright pink with blue drips running down them.

‘Oh snap!’ said Bluebell. ‘Don’t worry! I will try again!’

‘No!’ shouted Tobin and Billy in alarm.

Bluebell looked very surprised.

'Er... it's just that... er... it will be more fun to clean it all up together,' Tobin said.

'Really?' asked Bluebell.

'Most definitely!' replied Billy.

'Alright then!' said Bluebell, 'can you pass me a sponge.' She flew off into the dripping rainbow sky.

Billy puffed out his cheeks in relief and Tobin took off his bobble hat and wiped his head. Then he stuck the hat down firmly onto his ears.

'Right!' said Billy. 'Let's get this mess cleared up before anymore fairies come and try to help us.'

Tobin nodded and quickly began to scrub the nearest blue and pink splodged cloud!

Printed in Great Britain
by Amazon